SUPER RABBIT BOY
BLASTS OFF!

READ MORE
PRESS START!
BOOKS!

MORE BOOKS COMING SOON!

PRESS START!

SUPER RABBIT BOY
BLASTS OFF!

THOMAS
FLINTHAM

BRANCHES

SCHOLASTIC INC.

FOR GEMMA AND STEVE

Copyright © 2018 by Thomas Flintham

All rights reserved. Published by Scholastic Inc., *Publishers since 1920.* SCHOLASTIC, BRANCHES, and associated logos are trademarks and/or registered trademarks of Scholastic Inc.

The publisher does not have any control over and does not assume any responsibility for author or third-party websites or their content.

No part of this publication may be reproduced, stored in a retrieval system, or transmitted in any form or by any means, electronic, mechanical, photocopying, recording, or otherwise, without written permission of the publisher. For information regarding permission, write to Scholastic Inc., Attention: Permissions Department, 557 Broadway, New York, NY 10012.

This book is a work of fiction. Names, characters, places, and incidents are either the product of the author's imagination or are used fictitiously, and any resemblance to actual persons, living or dead, business establishments, events, or locales is entirely coincidental.

Library of Congress Cataloging-in-Publication Data

Name: Flintham, Thomas, author, illustrator. | Flintham, Thomas. Press start!
Title: Super Rabbit Boy blasts off! / by Thomas Flintham.
Description: First edition. | New York : Branches/Scholastic Inc., 2018. |
Series: Press start! ; 5 | Summary: King Viking decides to find another
planet where he can carry out his evil plans without interference, and
everyone in Animal Town is delighted; then an alien appeals to Super
Rabbit Boy for help and he blasts off to once again confront his
enemy—but his level one rocket may not be up to the task.
Identifiers: LCCN 2017048081 | ISBN 9781338239706 (hardcover) |
ISBN 9781338239621 (pbk.)
Subjects: LCSH: Superheroes—Juvenile fiction. | Supervillains—Juvenile
fiction. | Animals—Juvenile fiction. | Space ships—Juvenile fiction. |
Video games—Juvenile fiction. | CYAC: Superheroes—Fiction. |
Supervillains—Fiction. | Animals—Fiction. | Space ships—Fiction. |
Video games—Fiction.
Classification: LCC PZ7.1.F585 Sr 2018 | DDC [Fic]—dc23
LC record available at https://lccn.loc.gov/2017048081

19 18 17 16 15 14   23 24 25 26 27

Printed in India   197
First edition, August 2018
Edited by Celia Lee
Book design by Maria Mercado

TABLE OF CONTENTS

Buckle up! We'll be at Grandma and Grandpa's house in eight hours.
Eight hours!
Don't worry. Time will fly by!

1 PRESS START!

This is Animal Town. Hero Super Rabbit Boy and all his friends are having a party! Main meanie, King Viking, has gone away forever.

He left this letter for Super Rabbit Boy.

DEAR <u>STINKY</u> RABBIT BOY,

   I HAVE HAD ENOUGH.
YOU WIN! YOU ALWAYS RUIN
MY BEST PLANS AND BEAT MY
BEST ROBOTS. I AM MOVING AWAY.
   I AM BLASTING OFF INTO SPACE,
AND I AM NEVER COMING BACK. I WANT
TO BE FAR AWAY FROM YOU AND ALL
YOUR HAPPY FRIENDS.
   I HOPE YOU HAVE A BAD LIFE!

   YOURS SINCERELY,
   KING VIKING

P.S. I THINK SPACE WILL BE GREAT!

Everyone in Animal Town is so happy without King Viking! He won't destroy things ever again.

Suddenly, Celia Crocodile spots a spark in the sky.
Is that a shooting star?
No, it's a space rocket heading straight for Animal Town!
EEK!

The rocket lands. The animals are scared. Then, a green alien hops out!

Animal Town is shocked that King Viking is causing trouble in space. But Super Rabbit Boy is ready.

Don't worry, Glob Glorp! I can stop King Viking!

Really? Thank you so much!

Now, how will I get to space?

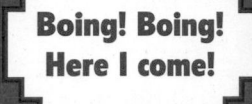

Super Rabbit Boy is in space. Stars and planets are everywhere.

Wow, space is amazing!

Super Rabbit Boy starts his search for King Viking. But the rocket moves slowly.

Suddenly, he spots action up ahead.

It's an army of King Viking's Rocket-Robos.

Super Rabbit Boy swoops into action.

He tests the laser on the zooming Rocket-Robos. They're hard to stop!

The Level 1 rocket has a very weak laser. But Super Rabbit Boy learns how to make it work.

BEEP!

I'm getting the hang of this!

He needs to get the Rocket-Robos three times each to stop them.

BOOP!

Super Rabbit Boy stops the final Rocket-Robo. The whole army has been beaten!

Did I beat all of them?

Super Rabbit Boy sees a flash in the distance.

Wait, what is that?

It's a giant Rocket-Robo Boss! The Boss is attacking a space station with its laser cannons!

Super Rabbit Boy is ready. But his Level 1 rocket is so weak. The Rocket-Robo Boss is stronger than the Rocket-Robos. Will he be able to defeat the Rocket-Robo Boss?

Super Rabbit Boy zooms toward the Rocket-Robo Boss!

The Rocket-Robo Boss fires its laser cannons at Super Rabbit Boy.

I will stop you, Super Rabbit Boy!

Super Rabbit Boy's Level 1 rocket is not very fast. But he still dodges the cannon blasts.

Super Rabbit Boy's laser finds the Rocket-Robo Boss. Nothing happens!

BOOP! BOOP! Your Level 1 laser is too weak for my Level 5 robot-armor!

20

Oh no! What can Super Rabbit Boy do? Suddenly, a voice calls out from the space station.

Super Rabbit Boy fires at the Rocket-Robo Boss's three glowing weak spots.

BOOP!

ZAP!

ZAP!

ZAP!

BEEP!

HOORAY!

You did it, Super Rabbit Boy!

The Flobs on the space station are happy!
They invite Super Rabbit Boy aboard to
thank him.

Soon, Super Rabbit Boy blasts off in search of King Viking. This time he's in a shiny, upgraded Level 2 rocket!

Super Rabbit Boy approaches a red planet.

Maybe I'll find some sign of King Viking here. . . .

Oh no! Another army of King Viking's Rocket-Robos is attacking the planet! Can Super Rabbit Boy save the red planet from King Viking's Rocket-Robo Army?

5 A BIG SURPRISE

Super Rabbit Boy swoops into action! His Level 2 rocket can stop each Rocket-Robo with just one blast!

BOOP!

Take that!

Super Rabbit Boy makes his way through the Rocket-Robo Army.

The Rocket-Robos try to fire back at Super Rabbit Boy. But he's too fast now! He zooms out of the way.

Super Rabbit Boy is good at flying his upgraded rocket. He speeds easily through the army of Rocket-Robos.

Super Rabbit Boy chases the last of the Rocket-Robos down toward the surface of the red planet.

The small Roo-Roos watch as they fly
toward them.

Don't worry!
I am here to help.

The Roo-Roos cheer as Super Rabbit Boy beats the last of the Rocket-Robos.

Suddenly, a huge shadow falls over the red planet.

Super Rabbit Boy circles around the giant Robo-U.F.O. He's looking for a weak spot. He can't find one. All of his blasts bounce off the armor.

BOOP! BOOP! My **Level 6** armor covers all my weak points. You can't beat me!

Super Rabbit Boy has an idea.

> I know what to do!

He flies straight into the Robo-U.F.O.'s mouth!

Inside, he finds a maze of pipes. Super Rabbit Boy twists and turns as he searches for a weak spot!

There must be a weak spot somewhere.

Super Rabbit Boy sees a glow in one corner. He zooms toward it.

It's a giant room with a giant glowing core.

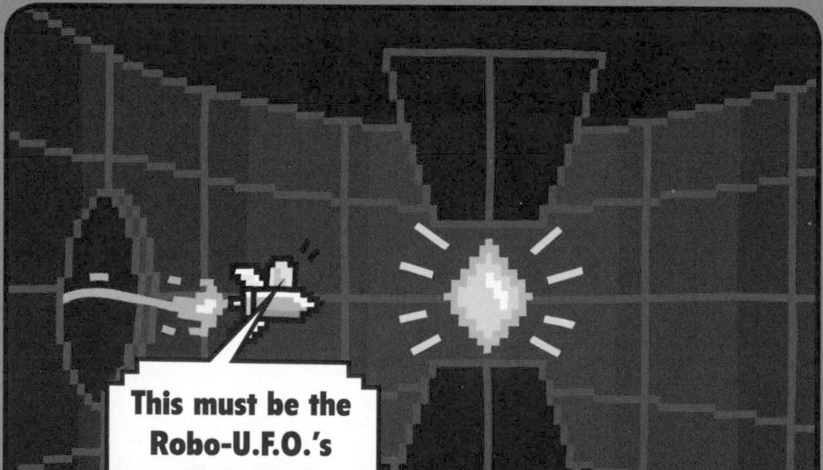

This must be the Robo-U.F.O.'s weak spot!

Super Rabbit Boy fires his laser at the glowing core.

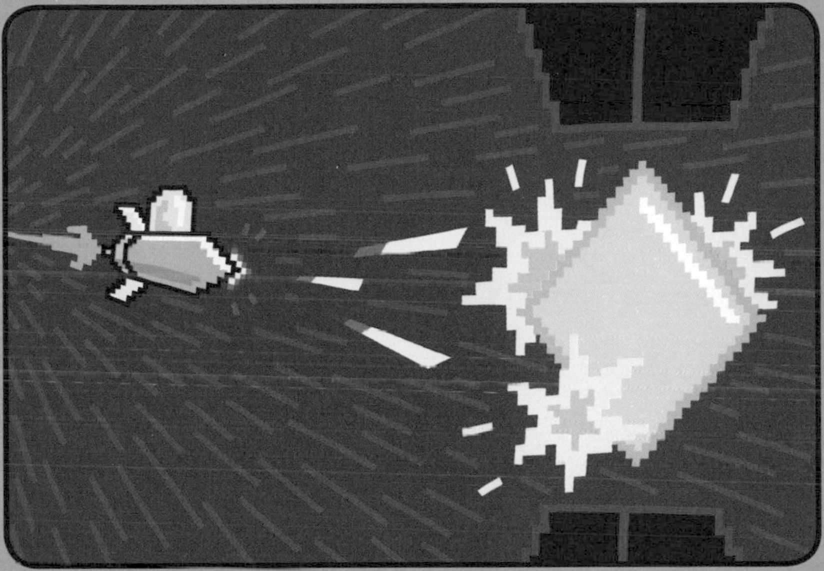

It takes a few tries, but the core breaks at last! The whole room starts to shake.

I better get out of here!

Super Rabbit Boy has to fly quickly back through the maze. Can he find his way out of the Robo-U.F.O. before it's too late?

Quick, Super Rabbit Boy!

7 THE BLUE MOON BLUES

Super Rabbit Boy's rocket flies out of the Robo-U.F.O. just in time! The Robo-U.F.O. explodes with a big bang!

BOOOOOOOP!

Good work, Super Rabbit Boy! You did it!

The Roo-Roos cheer! They are thankful, so they upgrade Super Rabbit Boy's rocket.

Now Super Rabbit Boy has a Level 3 rocket! He sets off once again to search for King Viking.

LEVEL 3

Super Rabbit Boy flies near a blue moon.
He spies some more Rocket-Robos.

He quickly blasts his way through the
army. The Level 3 laser really helps!

BEEP!

BOOP!

BEEP!

After the army, Super Rabbit Boy sees another Rocket-Robo Boss. It's attacking a moon base full of Moonies.

This Rocket-Robo Boss has super long arms. It tries to grab Super Rabbit Boy's rocket. Super Rabbit Boy uses his Level 3 rocketspeed to fly out of the way.

Super Rabbit Boy sees the Rocket-Robo Boss's glowing weak spot. He uses his laser.

The Rocket-Robo Boss blasts apart into many pieces!

I did it! Now I must find King Viking!

Oh no! How will Super Rabbit Boy ever catch up to and beat a Level 10 rocket?

8 THE SPACE CHASE

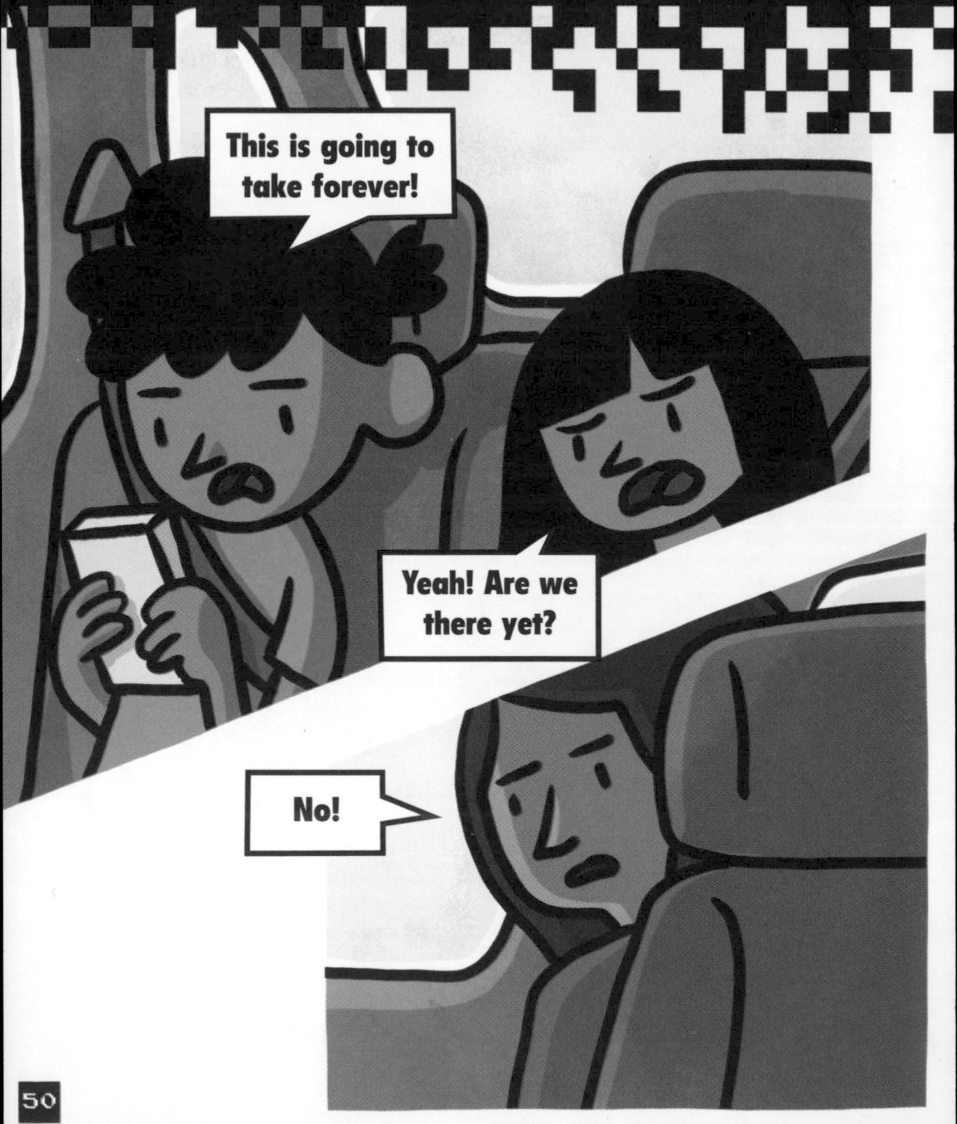

The Moonies thank Super Rabbit Boy for saving their moon base.

Moon! Moon! Hooray!

Moon! Moon! Yay!

They upgrade Super Rabbit Boy's rocket to thank him. Now it's at Level 4!

LEVEL 4

Super Rabbit Boy keeps searching for King Viking and upgrading his rocket. He stops any Rocket-Robos he finds.

BEEP!

Are we there now?

No!

He stops any Rocket-Robo Bosses, too.

BOOP!

Are we there yet?

No!

Everywhere Super Rabbit Boy goes, there are more Rocket-Robos. But he does not see any sign of King Viking.

Are we almost there now?

No!

Now?

No!

When Super Rabbit Boy saves people, they upgrade his rocket for him. Finally, he has a <u>Level 10</u> rocket! But he still hasn't found King Viking.

Where is he?

LEVEL 10

Now?

NO!!!

Now Super Rabbit Boy's search brings him to a space city. It is under attack by another Robo-U.F.O.

His Level 10 rocket is powerful! His laser goes straight through the Robo-U.F.O.'s armor in one blast!

Suddenly, someone taps Super Rabbit Boy on the back.

Yar! Excuse me, Super Rabbit Boy, I have a special gift for you!

Thank you! What is it?

Yar! It's my new machine! It can upgrade a rocket to Level 11!

Level 11? That means I'll be stronger than King Viking! Thank you!

Hooray! Keep going, Super Rabbit Boy!

9 SUPER SPEED

Super Rabbit Boy blasts off into space again. His Level 11 rocket is so fast! It moves at the speed of light.

I'll catch up with King Viking in no time!

LEVEL 11

Super Rabbit Boy finds a super big rocket zooming through space. Rocket-Robos fly out of the rocket toward him.

Super Rabbit Boy fires his Level 11 laser!

The Level 11 laser stops all the Rocket-Robos in one blast!

Captain Robo tells Super Rabbit Boy everything:

Glob Glorp was King Viking in disguise! He tricked Super Rabbit Boy into flying off into space on an endless journey. Then King Viking captured Animal Town while Super Rabbit Boy was busy in space!

Super Rabbit Boy is shocked. But he quickly jumps back into his rocket!

Can Super Rabbit Boy get back to Animal Town before it's too late?

HOMEWARD BOUND

Super Rabbit Boy blasts through space all the way back home.

King Viking is making trouble in Animal Town. He has a giant Level 10 Robo-U.F.O.

King Viking! You stinky trickster!

Super Rabbit Boy! What are you doing back?

Super Rabbit Boy blasts King Viking's Robo-U.F.O. with his Level 11 laser. King Viking goes flying. His plans have been ruined again.

Well done, Super Rabbit Boy. You saved Animal Town and space, too!

THOMAS FLINTHAM

has always loved to draw and tell stories, and now that is his job! He grew up in Lincoln, England, and studied illustration in Camberwell, London. He lives by the sea with his wife, Bethany, in Cornwall.

Thomas is the creator of Thomas Flintham's Book of Mazes and Puzzles and many other books for kids. PRESS START! is his first early chapter book series.

I'm going to find your core and put an end to your troublemaking!

Boop! You'll never find my core!

Can you help Super Rabbit Boy find a way to the Robo-U.F.O.'s core?